No More Victims

by

Natasha Cooper

First published in 2008 in Great Britain by
Barrington Stoke Ltd
18 Walker Street, Edinburgh, EH3 7LP

www.barringtonstoke.co.uk

ISBN: 978-1-84299-556-3

Printed in Great Britain by Bell & Bain Ltd

A Note from the Author

The idea for *No More Victims* came to me one day when I was thinking about people who cross the line and commit violent crime.

There are three boys in my story. One grows up seeing his mother beaten up again and again by his stepfather. One is so tough that no one dares to bully or hurt him. And one, who has just moved to the estate, is scared of everyone.

When one of the boys is attacked, all three families have to deal with fear and suspicion. It is not only their own feelings that make their lives so hard but also the way everyone else thinks about them.

Finding out what really happened, and who did it, was a real adventure for me. I hope it will be the same for you,

Natasha Cooper

In memory of my mother, who taught me to read when the school had failed.

With special thanks to our readers:

Simon Medcalf
Robert Napier
Lesley Oglesby

Contents

Prologue

The boy didn't know he was dying. Only that he was hurting. He tried to stand. But his legs were shaking so badly he couldn't get up. And he was cold.

He screwed up his scarf and held it against his jumper to keep the blood in. Soon he'd try to get up again, but he needed to rest first. All he could see were the dirty brick walls and the big black rubbish bins.

The stink from the bins was horrible, like rotting vegetables mixed with piss. A cat slid by, brushing his hand with its fur.

He could hear people talking and laughing. But they didn't hear him when he called out for help. Or else they didn't care.

His eyes were flickering, and his teeth were banging against each other as he shivered. They hurt. His front hurt. Everything hurt. He couldn't breathe.

Someone was coming.

"Help." His voice didn't come out right, so he tried to shout, but that made the pain worse. It felt like sharp fingers digging into him. "Help."

His voice was still too low, but he thought someone must have heard him because the foot-steps came nearer and nearer. The boy felt a bit better and tried to get up again.

Then he heard Terry's voice, so he curled up into a ball to hide his face. He didn't want Terry knowing he was here. He didn't want Terry near him, ever again.

But Terry came anyway and crashed down on the ground. His hands were heavy, and they hurt as they pulled away the scarf. The boy fought back, but he couldn't keep Terry off him.

And then Terry's voice boomed out again.

"Fucking hell!"

Chapter 1
Rush Hour

The roar of the lorries was all Candy could hear as she rode home on her bike in the dark, beside the River Thames. Her legs were tired as she pumped the pedals.

A man who was talking into his phone stepped out in front of her without looking.

"Stupid bitch," he shouted as she tried to squeeze between him and the high white side of a lorry.

"Sorry," Candy called out, although it wasn't her fault.

Her front wheel caught in a pot-hole and nearly threw her off the bike. The traffic was always bad at this time in the afternoon. But at least there was no rain or snow to slow her up, even though it was January.

Candy had been late leaving the office because her boss had made her correct yet more of *his* mistakes. Her twelve-year-old son, Adam, would be home before her and that didn't seem right on the first day of term. Not when he'd spent all the Christmas holidays working on the anti-bullying tricks his grandfather had taught him.

The lorry was getting closer as the traffic surged towards the crossroads by the bridge. The lorry's left indicator started flashing. Either the driver hadn't looked in his mirror or he reckoned a woman on a bike didn't matter. If he didn't stop squeezing her, she'd be tipped on to the pavement.

He didn't stop. Candy jammed on her brakes and heard a curse from a man on a bike behind her. He almost ran into her. The ugly great lorry turned left to cross the bridge and she looked over her shoulder to make sure the man behind her understood why she'd stopped so suddenly. He looked like an earwig in his tight black Lycra clothes. He scowled at her.

By the time the lorry was gone, the traffic lights had changed. The man who looked like an earwig charged past her, going right through the red light. Candy waited, like the patient woman she was.

When the lights turned green, she set off again. Last term, Adam had come home every day with ripped-up books, torn clothes and dark blue-grey bruises all over his body. But at breakfast this morning he'd promised her he wasn't going to be a victim any more.

Now another vast lorry was over-taking Candy, sending fumes up her nose and dust into her eyes. She didn't have much further to go. She hoped Adam would be all right until she got home.

She heard a siren. Soon an ambulance passed her, followed by two police cars. For a minute she was sure they must have been called out to rescue Adam, then she saw the ambulance turning right well before her flat. This time it must be OK. This time it couldn't have been Adam who'd been hurt.

She crossed the road, lifted the bike over the pavement and walked into the estate.

The climb up to her fifth-floor flat, carrying the bike, was hard but it had to be done. Only a mug would chain up a bike at ground level and expect it to have wheels in the morning.

There was no light coming from the flat.

Candy let herself rest half-way up the stairs. If Adam wasn't home, she didn't need to rush. When she'd got her breath back, she'd go on up the steps.

But as her breathing got easier and her heart stopped banging so loudly she began to worry. Why wasn't he back? Had the bullies got him again?

The dark windows of the flat were like mirrors and she saw herself reflected in them. Dirty from the car fumes, with her blonde hair in a mess, she looked awful, and worrying had given her lines no woman of 30 should have.

She chained the bike to the black mesh fence and let herself into the flat. There wasn't much furniture yet. A small round pine table took up one corner of the living room, with four matching chairs. Two sofas stood on the opposite side of the room. The walls were white, and the carpet was dark blue. There were no pictures.

For a while she stood in front of the balcony doors, trying to forget that Adam was now half an hour late. From here she could see the river and the park on the far side. The lights and the bare trees and the dark water were better than any picture.

But they didn't stop her worrying.

Half an hour later, she couldn't bear it any longer. She knew she'd have to go and look for him, even if it made him angry. He'd told her last term that he never wanted her anywhere near the school because she made him look like a baby and that made the bullying worse.

She picked up her keys and went out into the little hall. Then she heard his voice. He was laughing. All that worry had been for nothing. He was all right. The bullies hadn't got him this time. She waited for him to unlock the door, but he didn't. Then she heard the sound of a cup hitting a saucer as he laughed again.

The sounds were coming through the wall between her flat and the one next door. He must be there, having tea with his friend Mike and Mike's mum, Tanya.

Relieved, but feeling stupid about her fretting, Candy went to knock on their door so she could join the party.

Chapter 2
The Visit

"Hi," said Tanya, opening the door. She was wearing black cargo pants and a red jumper. "Come and have tea," she said, tucking a stray wisp of her dark hair into the rubber band that held the rest swinging high up on the back of her head. "There's some cake left."

"Thanks." Candy smiled at her.

If it hadn't been for Tanya, the six months Candy and Adam had spent on the estate would have been even harder.

Candy followed Tanya into the warm, untidy room and saw both boys with cans of

Coke in their hands, watching the huge flat-screen TV.

"Hi, Adam!" Candy said. "Mike."

Adam turned and grinned at her. He waved his Coke can, too. And Mike nodded at her in greeting.

Candy was glad to see that there were no rips in Adam's clothes, even though they were so dirty they looked as if he'd been rolling in the road outside.

Tanya gave her a plate with a large slab of cake on it. Taking a big bite made it easier for Candy to keep all her questions to herself.

As she finished the last of the cake, she realised she could hear a lot of noise outside. Heavy feet were trampling up and down and voices were calling out to one another. They sounded official – urgent, too. Tanya shouted from the kitchen, "What's happening out there?"

Candy listened more carefully. She thought back to what she'd seen as she biked home and said, "I saw an ambulance on my way home, with police cars following it. Maybe there's been an accident. A hit-and-run or something like that."

Out of the corner of her eye she saw the two boys glance at each other, then Adam turned away. He seemed scared, which puzzled Candy. Mike didn't show any signs of fear, but there weren't many things – or people – that frightened him.

In fact, Candy thought, *today he's looking mean enough to scare off anyone who got in his way.*

Someone knocked on the door before she could ask the boys what was going on between them. Tanya went to open it and came back with a young red-haired police officer in uniform.

"This is PC Edwards," she said. "He wants to talk to us all. I'll make more tea."

"Not for me, thanks," said PC Edwards, as he took off his cap and tucked it under his arm.

He was holding a clipboard with a list of questions on it.

"That looks like trouble," Candy said, worried. She pointed to the list. "What's happened?"

"You'd better all sit down," PC Edwards said.

There wasn't room for all of them on the sofa, so Mike stayed standing. He leaned against the wall by the TV, glaring at Adam.

Mike was only a few months older than Adam, but he was much bigger and stronger. He had a quick temper too, and there were people at school who liked seeing him lose it. Last term, when the bullies hadn't been going at Adam, they'd been ganging up on Mike, until he blew up and hit someone. Then he'd been the one to get in trouble, instead of them.

"Can I have your names, please?" said PC Edwards.

Tanya answered first, then Candy gave him her details and Adam's. PC Edwards wrote everything down. He went a bit pink when he had to ask how to spell Candy's surname. He had to cross out what he'd written and start again.

"I think he fancies you," whispered Tanya to Candy.

When he'd got everything down on the form, PC Edwards asked what they'd all been doing since the end of school.

"What *is* all this?" Candy asked. "Has there been an accident?"

PC Edwards nodded, but he wouldn't tell them who'd been hurt, or how. Tanya said she'd been at home in the flat ever since she'd done her shopping in the morning. Then it was the boys' turn. Candy watched Adam's face flood with colour as he mumbled something she couldn't hear.

"Adam?" she said, worried all over again.

He looked at the floor, shaking his head. Even more worried, she looked over at Mike, who was still standing by the TV. He wouldn't meet her gaze either.

"Adam?" said PC Edwards, holding his pen over the list on his clipboard.

"Yeah," said Adam, still staring at the floor.

He was hunched over, nibbling at his lower lip. He looked just like the kind of wimp who'd make any bully pick on him. Candy wanted to remind him he'd sworn not to be a victim any more.

"Did you come right home from school?" asked PC Edwards. He sounded kind enough, but it didn't help Adam answer.

He shook his head again. His hands were clenching and unclenching at his sides.

He must have seen it happen, Candy thought. Whatever "it" was. She knew what happened to grasses on this estate as well as he did. No wonder he seemed so scared.

But she didn't know how to help him, so she just said his name. Adam kept his face turned away, so she couldn't tell what he was thinking. Mike grinned at her, as though he was trying to reassure her, then he looked at PC Edwards.

"We didn't see any ..." Mike began.

"I'll come to you later," said PC Edwards. "I want Adam to tell me first. Adam, what did you do after school?"

At last Adam felt in the pocket of his grey school trousers and pulled out a packet of cigarettes. He looked at Candy with great huge eyes full of worry and apology.

"Mike and I went to the shop and I got these," he said. "Sorry, Mum."

Candy hated smoking. And she hated Adam breaking the law by buying cigarettes at his age. But at least now she knew what was making him look so frightened. And it could have been a lot worse.

"Where did you get the cash?" she asked, knowing he'd spent all his pocket money last weekend.

Adam gave a shiver as though he'd been dumped in a freezer. *Oh, not thieving*, Candy thought. *Please not thieving.*

She hated everything this place was doing to him. And she hated her husband for dumping her so that she'd had to bring Adam to live here.

"I took it from your tin in the kitchen," Adam said, speaking freely at last. "Sorry, Mum."

"It's OK," Candy said, relieved in a way because taking her money wasn't nearly as bad as stealing anyone else's. "Just this once. PC Edwards, what has happened?"

"There's been an assault. Kind of."

He wouldn't tell them any more, but he asked if any of them knew a family called Jackson.

Candy felt her guts relax at once, as though someone had flicked a switch to free them. If this assault involved the Jackson family, she could stop worrying.

"Of course we do," Tanya said. "They live on the other side of the estate. Mary Jackson has a son called Ben, who's in the same class as Mike and Adam. But it's Mary's boyfriend, Terry, who's the problem. He's a violent bastard. Was the ambulance for her? Has he been hitting her again?"

"Sounds as if you know them well," said PC Edwards.

"Yeah," Tanya said. "Well, we know Mary and Ben, anyway. And we've heard all about Terry."

"Does he ever hit Ben?" said PC Edwards.

"No," said Tanya. "Only Mary."

"So who does hit Ben?" asked PC Edwards, looking first at Tanya and Candy, then at the two boys.

Adam pulled out his fags again, then saw his mother glaring at him and put them back in his pocket.

"He gets in fights at school sometimes," said Mike. "I heard someone call him a snivelling little tosser at the end of last term, and he found the guts to kick out."

"Who did?" said PC Edwards, alert now and clicking the top of his biro over and over again. "Who did he kick?"

Mike shuffled his feet and said he didn't know. Adam was picking at his nails, so focused that it was clear he hoped no one would ask him anything about the incident.

"OK," PC Edwards said at last. "You can't have been the only one who saw it. We'll get the name from one of the others."

"Is Ben badly hurt?" Candy asked.

"All I know is, it's an assault," said PC Edwards, looking away.

It was the TV that told them the truth. The main news was over and now it was the local reports. Tanya turned up the sound.

"*A twelve-year-old boy has been stabbed to death ...*"

Chapter 3
Wounds

The forensics team had done their work in Mary Jackson's flat, and DS Jim Smith was hoping to interview her. At the moment she was lying in bed with her mashed-up face turned to the wall, while a doctor cleaned up a long, jagged cut on her arm.

DS Smith stood in the little hallway, looking into the kitchen. There was still blood everywhere. It lay in a pool on the black and white floor and there were splashes up over the white units.

Forensics had taken samples for the lab, but it would be days before they could say for sure whose blood it was. Most of it must be Mary's, but some could have come from Ben.

If it had, then there'd be no problem making the court believe that Ben had been stabbed in here. And that would help prove Terry was lying when he said he hadn't seen Ben until he'd found him dying by the bins outside.

DS Smith knew Terry was lying about that as well as everything else, but he also knew what lawyers were like. If you didn't tie everything up tight, they would argue all your evidence away.

If the CCTV camera near the bins hadn't been smashed, that would have given them everything they needed to make the charge stick. As it was, they'd have to rely on house-to-house interviews and any other evidence they could pick up.

Smith had seen a set of knives in a wooden block on the kitchen work-top. One knife was missing. It would have been just about the right size to make the wound in Ben's chest.

Smith went into the kitchen, taking care to step over the blood on the floor, and searched all the drawers and cupboards. There was no sign of the knife anywhere.

The doctor came out of Mary's room and said to Smith, "You can go in now. You may not get much out of her. But she is fit enough to talk."

Mary was lying on top of the pink duvet on the double bed, still wearing her bloody clothes. Jim was shocked by the sight of her face, even now the doctor had cleaned it up.

There were stitches in the long cut in her cheek and a big bandage on her left arm. There were dark bruises all over her skin. And her lower lip was split.

Smith sat on the end of the bed, and said, "Hi, Mary. How are you feeling?"

She blinked, but she didn't say anything.

Smith tried again. "I know it hurts and you want to rest. But there are questions I have to ask. OK?"

A moment later she nodded. She winced, as though even moving her head made it hurt.

He said, "Terry did this to you, didn't he?"

Mary closed her eyes and didn't say a word. Smith tried to think of a way to help her talk.

He said, "You know Terry's making a statement down at the police station now, don't you? He's not here in the flat at the moment. He can't hear you."

Mary's eyes opened. She whispered, "Great." But her voice was flat, as if she thought it was anything but. And it was clear she wasn't going to say anything else.

Smith said, "We need to know what happened here today."

She pointed to the long raw wound in her face. The stitches made it look as though a railway line was crossing her skin.

Smith said, "Not just that, Mary. We need to know what happened to Ben."

Big fat tears were oozing out of her eyes. Smith felt very sorry for her, but he had to keep on with his questions.

"Did Ben come back from school today and see Terry beating you?"

Mary just looked at him, without saying anything. Smith knew he was making everything worse for her, but he had to do it.

He said, "You've got a set of knives in the kitchen, haven't you? Sharp ones."

Mary said, "Yes." Her voice sounded as if her throat hurt too. Had Terry been strangling her as well as everything else?

"The smallest knife's missing," Smith said. "Do you know where it is?"

Mary shook her head and winced again. Then her eyes closed and he knew she was hiding something. It was clear she was scared of Terry, but she had to tell the truth. Otherwise Terry would walk free again.

DS Smith stood up and moved nearer to the head of the bed.

"Mary, I need to know," he said. His voice sounded harsh in his own ears. He tried to make it more gentle when he went on, "When did you last see the knife?"

She turned her face towards the wall. He thought he had no hope of getting her to say any more.

Then she muttered something. He couldn't hear, so he bent closer and asked her to repeat it.

"I can't remember," she whispered. "I didn't know it was missing."

Smith was sure Ben had come back from school, seen Terry hitting her and tried to make him stop. What Smith didn't know was whether it was Ben or Terry who'd picked up the knife first, and that would make a difference to the court.

Ben was so small he couldn't have fought Terry on his own. Maybe he'd grabbed the knife so he'd have something to use as a threat. Terry wouldn't have had any trouble getting it off him, and, with a temper like Terry's, anything could have happened then. But if that was how it had happened, Terry would be able to claim it had been an accident.

"Have you tried Ben's room?" Mary said in a low whisper. "Maybe the knife's in there."

DS Smith went to look. Unlike the rest of the flat, Ben's bedroom was tidy. There were a few books neatly lined up on the shelves. The forensics team had finished checking the flat, but Smith still pulled on a pair of thin rubber gloves to make sure he didn't leave his prints on anything. Then he searched each of the three drawers below the bookshelf and looked in the cupboard.

He could see only clean clothes and a row of shoes on the floor. Ben must have out-grown lots of the shoes years ago, but he'd kept them all. Did it make him feel safer to have all his old things around him like this?

DS Smith lay down on the floor. There was nothing to be seen under the bed, not even any dust. He stood up again and pulled back the red and blue rug that covered the bed. He prodded the duvet with his hands. Still nothing.

But the pillow felt odd. There was something in it that was harder than the stuffing. Smith felt inside the pillow case.

Then he dragged the pillow itself out of the case and squeezed his fingers all along its seams. He found a gap in the seam. Pushing his hand in amongst the stuffing, he felt a thin book. How had forensics missed this?

When he'd got the book out, he saw it had grey paper covers, with the rusty marks of blood around one edge. Pushing one gloved finger gently between the pages to open it, he saw a child's writing. He began to read.

"Mum's head was bleeding this time. I tried to stop him hitting her more. But I'm not big enough yet."

The same kind of message came over and over again. The book told a story no boy of Ben's age should know anything about. If Smith had had Terry in front of him now, he'd have had hard work to stop himself battering the bastard to a pulp.

Chapter 4

Protection

Candy woke in the night to hear a scraping noise. She looked at the clock. Two-thirty. She'd had only an hour's sleep and she was very tired. The alarm clock would ring in another four hours. If she was going to get any work done during the day, she'd have to sleep again now.

Turning the pillow over, she lay face down and shut her eyes. The scraping sound came again. She raised her head and listened.

For a minute all she could hear were normal noises – the hum of traffic from outside, the hiss and bubble from the water pipes, a few distant shouts. Then the sound came again, a scraping or sawing that sounded as though someone was cutting through metal.

She got out of bed and put her old shawl around her. Whatever the noise was, it didn't sound like a threat, but she had to find out. When she'd pushed open her bedroom door as quietly as she could, she padded into the corridor in bare feet to Adam's room. It was empty.

She went on into the living room. The french doors to the balcony were open.

Outside, Adam was standing with the moonlight shining on his blond hair. His right arm moved backwards and forwards along the edge of the balcony. Each time he moved, the thing he had in his hands made the same scraping sound.

Candy moved quietly in case he was sleep-walking. She said, "What are you doing?"

She was so cold she tugged the shawl tightly around her bare arms.

"Sharpening the knife Dad gave me," Adam said, turning round to face her.

His blue eyes were stretched wide, and he looked very young in his old dressing gown with the twisted cord around his waist.

He added, "I'll need it to protect me now Ben's been killed."

Candy thought of lots of different words she might use and knew they would all be wrong.

"Adam, most people are hurt *because* they're carrying weapons," she said at last. "It's much safer not to have one."

She knew the blade of this pen-knife was tiny. The whole thing was so small it used to hang on her ex-husband's key ring. She thought any attacker would laugh at it. It couldn't protect Adam at all.

She said, "Give it here."

Adam said, "I *need* it."

Candy held out her hand. She said, "We've both had a bad day. And tomorrow isn't going to be any easier. We need our sleep. Give me the knife and get back to bed. We can talk about it all in the morning."

Adam turned with his back to the concrete balcony, holding the knife behind him. Candy was easily strong enough to take it away, but she didn't want to hurt him. The school bullies had done enough of that already.

Even at this hour traffic was still streaming along the road below the balcony. And the full moon hung so low that it looked very close behind him in the dark sky.

"Come on, Adam," she said. "Give it to me."

His eyes filled with tears, but they didn't fall. "I *need* it," he insisted. "To protect me."

"Believe me, you don't. Come on, give it here."

In the end, he did hold out the knife, but the look on his face made Candy think he'd never forgive her.

Even so, she took the knife from him. She put her right palm flat against the blunt edge of the blade to fold it up. It wouldn't move.

She looked down and saw that Adam had wound black tape around the hinge to keep the blade open.

"Oh, Adam, this is so risky," she said. "Go on back to bed, while I sort it out."

"It's *your* fault," he shouted. "If Dad was here I wouldn't need it."

Adam ran back towards his room. Candy didn't even try to work out why he thought it was her fault his dad had dumped them. Instead she set about peeling the black tape off the knife.

The first few circles came off easily, but the closer she got to the hinge, the stickier the tape seemed. She picked at it with her finger-nails and the blade slipped, cutting deep into the loose skin between her left thumb and the first finger.

Adam had made the blade horribly sharp.

Candy sucked away the blood, which tasted thin and metallic as well as salty, then she went back to stripping off the tape. She was working more carefully now. Every few seconds she had to stop to suck away more blood. At last, she'd got rid of all the tape and closed the knife.

Rain started to fall. It was so heavy that her hair was wet in seconds. She went back inside and looked for the plasters so she could cover the cut in her hand.

Chapter 5

Interrogation

DS Smith was in the small interview room at the police station. Terry sat on the other side of the table, with the duty solicitor. The walls of the room were the colour of stale cream and the hard chairs a grubby orange.

Smith said, "Come on. Just tell me why one of Mary's kitchen knives is missing."

Terry was angry. He said, "How the fuck do I know? Do I have anything to do with the fucking kitchen? Of course not. I never seen the fucking knife. You'll have to ask that lazy fucking cow what she's done with it."

"You mashed up her face so badly she doesn't feel like telling us anything right now," Smith said.

"I never," said Terry. "She must've tripped over her stupid feet and fell on her face. I wasn't even there. I was out, looking for Ben."

DS Smith knew it was a stupid lie. Anyone could see what Terry had done to Mary. He had bruises all over his right hand from where he'd hit her. Smith thought of all the things he'd like to call Terry. Wanker. Tosser. Scrote. Bastard. Animal.

"I thought I was here to give you a statement about how I found Ben bleeding to death. Why are you asking about fucking Mary?"

Smith gave a sigh, then he said, "OK, so let's talk about Ben. He came back from school and saw you hitting her, didn't he?"

Terry shook his head, saying, "I told you, I found him by the bins. I couldn't stand listening to Mary cry and whine about how she wanted him, so I went out to look, didn't I? And I found him by the bins, crying and whining just like his mum."

Smith was determined to get the truth. He said, "After you hit her, you mean."

It took lots of work, but at last Terry said, "OK, so I may have pushed her a bit before she fell. She was pissing me off. I didn't mean to hurt her and if she wasn't so clumsy she wouldn't have tripped. I just wanted her to shut the fuck up. Then after she fell she wanted Ben, so I went out to look for him."

DS Smith was still sure Ben had been in the flat while Terry'd been beating Mary, but he played along for a bit. "And how was Ben when you found him?"

Terry rubbed his hands up and down his shirt. It was the same colour as his cropped hair.

He said, "I already told you. Someone had stabbed him but he was still alive, whimpering and bleeding. I called the ambulance for him, like anyone would've."

Smith said, "If it wasn't you who stabbed him, who was it?"

Terry gave a shrug and said, "Must have been someone from school. They were always laughing at him and taking his stuff. Maybe it went too far this time."

"OK," said Smith. "Then tell me who they are and we'll talk to them."

Terry gave him the names of four boys, all older than Ben.

"OK," Smith said. "You can go."

Smith would have liked to arrest Terry, but that would have to come later, when there was proof that he was responsible for Mary's injuries. Or at least a statement from her.

"But we'll be watching," Smith went on. "And if you lay a finger on Mary again – ever – we'll know."

When Terry had gone, Smith went upstairs to report to his senior officer, DCI Sue Blake.

Her office was much brighter than the interview room. There was a big flower-pot of white Christmas roses on the window-sill.

DCI Blake was short and thin, not much bigger than a child. But her hard grey eyes were those of an adult who'd seen everything and hated most of it.

She didn't smile at Smith. She didn't often smile at anyone. But her voice was friendly when she asked Smith what Terry had told him.

"A bunch of lies, guv. He says someone at Ben's school must have stabbed him. He's given me four names. Here they are. I don't believe a word of it myself."

DCI Blake said, "You may be right. But we'll have to make sure. I'll get someone to bring these boys in. And we need to find that knife."

Smith said, "Anyone gone through the bins yet?"

DCI Blake nodded. "But they haven't found anything. If I was him, I'd have dropped it in the river or down one of the drains. In this rain, it would have been washed out to sea by now. It's been pissing down since last night."

"So where do we go from here?" Smith said.

"You'd better see what you can get from those women who told PC Edwards they knew Ben and Mary well," said DCI Blake. "OK?"

"Sure." Smith turned away, but DCI Blake's steely voice stopped him.

"One more thing," she said.

He waited.

Slowly and clearly, she said, "PC Edwards said that one of the women was something special. Remember, she could be a witness and be careful. We don't want any more trouble."

Smith didn't answer. Once, just once, a long time ago, he had started seeing a woman involved in a murder investigation. They had had to drop the case in the end. They said no one would trust the woman's evidence if they knew she was screwing a cop who was involved.

Smith never made the same mistake twice. Not about anything. He thought this woman could be like Cameron Diaz and he still wouldn't touch her. He left the DCI's office without another word.

Chapter 6
At First Sight

When Candy and Tanya got back to the flats from shopping, they saw a man standing by the steps. He was tall, well-built, with bright eyes. His dark hair was waxed into little peaks, and he was wearing black jeans and a tatty old leather jacket. He had a lively, good-looking face that made Candy think he could be an actor. And he was about her own age.

Tanya said, "Are you waiting for us?"

The man stood up and pulled out his warrant card. "I'm DS Smith. Can I have a word?"

Candy said to Smith, "Is this about Ben Jackson?"

"That's right," Smith said. "And his mum, Mary. I wanted to ask you both a few more questions, after what you said to PC Edwards. OK?"

Candy nodded and said they'd better go into her flat so they wouldn't be over-heard by Mike and Adam who were next door playing on the computer.

When they got inside she went to put the kettle on, while Tanya led Smith into the living room. Tanya took one of the sofas, but Smith pulled out a hard pine chair and sat on that. He was working – he couldn't relax.

Tanya said, "Have you charged Terry yet?"

Smith rubbed his chin. "Not yet. We haven't got enough evidence. That's why I'm here. I need anything you can tell me about the family."

Candy was filling the kettle. She splashed some water on her hand.

"Sod it," she said, drying her hand against her shirt. She looked at the dark smear the water had made. She thought of one time when she'd seen Mary with blood bubbling through her jumper.

If only Mary had let them tell the police about Terry then! Still angry with her for making them promise not to say anything about him, Candy jammed the lid on the kettle. She could see into the living room over the kitchen work-top.

"Hasn't Mary told you what happened in her flat yesterday?" Candy said. "She's the only person who really knows what Terry does."

"She won't talk," Smith said, turning to smile at Candy.

His eyes crinkled at the corners, she noticed. She had to look away so she could force herself to focus on his question.

No, she thought. *Mary's never talked frankly to anyone. If she had, Ben wouldn't be dead now.*

"I'm not surprised," Tanya said from the sofa, making Candy jump and snapping her out of her day-dream. "She's scared. Terry's told her often enough that he'll kill her if she ever says anything to anyone."

Candy got the milk from the fridge and the sugar for Tanya.

"But she's a good mother," Candy said. "I don't think she'd have stood by and watched Terry hurt Ben without calling for help, whatever she let Terry do to her. It must've been somebody else who killed Ben."

"You could be right," said Smith.

Candy thought how different he was from her shit of a husband, who'd always enjoyed

47

making her feel like a fool, even when he was wrong. Especially when he was wrong.

"But while I'm here, can I ask you a few more questions?" Smith went on.

"Of course," Candy said. "We'll tell you anything we can."

The kettle boiled and she made the tea. As Smith took the mug she offered him, she noticed how strong his hands were, and how clean his nails.

"Thanks," he said, smiling again. "That looks great. Were either of you ever in Mary's kitchen?"

Candy took a gulp of tea and swallowed quickly because it was so hot. She felt the burn all down her throat and into her chest. When the heat had faded a bit, she coughed and said, "I was there, taking in some shopping I'd done for her, only last weekend."

"Lucky her," Smith said, looking at Candy as if they'd known each other for years.

She wished they had. She had an idea that she'd be able to tell him anything, even the bad stuff she'd never shared with Tanya about how much she'd hated her husband. And how she didn't know how to help Adam now he'd gone and left them. And how she dreaded hearing Adam cry out in the night because of his bad dreams. And how scared he was all the time at school, even when he was trying to look tough.

Smith was waiting, not even trying to hurry her. It was almost as though he could hear what she was thinking and wanted to give her time to get her ideas in order.

In the end, he said, "Try to remember Mary's kitchen as you saw it when you took the shopping in."

Candy tried to focus. "OK," she said.

"What did you see on the work-top between the sink and the cooker?"

"Jars of tea bags and sugar," she said. "An oven glove. Some pots of salt and pepper. The knife set."

Smith asked her to describe the knife set.

"The knives were stainless steel, with black plastic handles."

"How many were there?" Smith said.

"There should have been six. But the slot for the smallest one was empty, so there were only five."

Smith said, "Are you sure?"

Candy felt sick as she understood what he was thinking, and what she ought to tell him now, and why she didn't want to.

"Yes," she said, hoping her voice didn't give anything away. "Why?"

"We think that's what was used to stab Ben. But we're not sure."

"But ..." Candy began before Tanya stopped her.

"The little knife was in the block yesterday morning," Tanya said in a very sure kind of voice. Her dark pony-tail swung from side to side as she tossed her head.

"How do you know?" Smith asked.

She said, "I was doing some washing up for Mary and I put the knife in the block myself. It was only yesterday morning. Must have been about ten o'clock. Before I did my shopping."

Candy didn't say anything. She couldn't. Tanya had lied. They both knew what had happened to the smallest knife in the set, and it didn't have anything to do with Ben's death. Mary had broken the blade weeks ago, when she'd tried to use it as a screwdriver. Tanya herself had taken it to throw it in the bins on her way home so that Terry would never find out what Mary had done. If he'd used a knife to stab Ben, it must have been a different one.

Smith said, "Will you sign a statement about seeing the knife in the block?"

"Of course," Tanya said. "Whenever you want."

Smith looked at Candy. "What about you? Will you sign a statement?"

"But I wasn't there," Candy said. "So I didn't see it. So I can't pretend I did."

She drank some more tea. It was cooler now, easier to swallow. And it gave her an excuse to look away.

Smith undid his leather jacket. He was wearing a shirt under it, too loose to show off his muscles, but she knew they were there.

Changing the subject, Smith said, "Tell me about the bullies who made Ben's life hell. PC Edwards said he had a hard time at school, just like your Adam does."

Candy said, "That's right."

Tanya got up off the sofa so she could put her hand on Candy's arm. It felt very comforting.

"Adam fought back," Tanya said. "He wasn't a wimp like Ben, who nearly always ran away and hid. Adam always stood up to everyone, however hard it was. That's why he gets hurt."

Smith's phone rang. He looked at the screen, then put the phone back in his pocket. He said, "I've got to go. Will you phone me if you think of anything else I need to know?"

Tanya laughed and tossed back her pony-tail again. "We would if we had your number, wouldn't we, Candy?"

Smith wrote it down for them, but it was Candy he gave the piece of paper to, just letting his fingers touch hers as he handed it over.

Chapter 7
Arrest

When Smith left Candy's flat, he walked across the estate to Mary's block. There weren't many people around. Maybe they were all staying at home because they were afraid of whoever had killed Ben.

The first thing Smith heard when he reached Mary's grey front door was Terry's voice, shouting inside the flat.

"You stupid fucking cow. Why didn't you tell the cops what I told you to say? You should have said I never touched Ben. Why can't you ever get anything right, you stupid cow?"

Smith banged hard on the door. Terry's voice got lower, but it didn't stop altogether. Somehow his whispers were worse than the yelling. Smith knocked on the door again a bit more softly.

After a few seconds, Mary opened the door. She was scared and the railway-track scars on her face looked awful. But there weren't any new ones and the bruises were yellow round the edges. It didn't look as though Terry had hit her again since he got out of the police custody.

Smith reminded Mary who he was and asked if he could come in. She opened the door a little wider. Smith went in and saw Terry standing in the kitchen with his back to the sink.

Terry said, "What the fuck do you want now?"

Smith walked right in front of Terry and said, "I want to make sure Mary's OK. And then I want to ask her some questions."

Terry said, "Then ask the stupid cow. She won't be able to tell you anything because she's too thick. But you can always try."

Smith turned and saw that Mary's face was blank, as though she didn't dare let anyone see how she felt. Smith took her into her bedroom and closed the door so Terry couldn't threaten her. Then Smith told her what Tanya had said about the little knife.

He sat on the edge of her bed and went on, "Is Tanya right, Mary? Was the little knife in the block yesterday morning?"

Mary nodded her head. Then she licked her split lips. They looked very sore.

Smith said, "And did Terry use it to hurt Ben?"

Mary took much longer to respond this time. She went on licking her lips. Sometimes she looked round as though she needed to be sure Terry was not in the room with them.

At last, she whispered, "I think so."

Smith thanked her. Then he left her safely in her bedroom and went back into the kitchen.

He told Terry he was arresting him for the murder of Ben Jackson.

Terry thumped both hands on the kitchen cupboard behind him, swearing and yelling. Smith gave him a caution.

Terry spat into the sink. Then he said, "This is all Mary's stupid fault. Her and those bitches Candy and Tanya. None of them can keep their mouths shut. Stupid fucking bitches."

Chapter 8

Secrets And Lies

Candy was washing up the tea mugs, wishing it was DS Smith sitting in her living room and not Tanya. By the time she'd dried everything up and put it all away, she knew she had to tackle Tanya.

"Why did you lie about the knife?" she said.

Tanya looked up from her magazine and said, "Why didn't you? It was the best thing to do. This'll get Terry out of Mary's life at last. She'll be OK while he's in prison. And he should go down for a long time."

"But what if he didn't kill Ben?" Candy said. "Tanya, haven't you thought of that?"

Tanya gave a shrug, which made her top rise up above her cargo pants. Candy could see the silver ring in her belly button.

Tanya said, "Am I bothered? He deserves it for what he's done to Mary all these months. And someone has to pay for Ben's death. Terry's as good a person as anyone else."

She looked back at her magazine, pretending not to care but breathing so fast her breasts were hardly ever still. Candy had only known her for a few months, but it was long enough to understand this: Tanya was scared, which must mean that she knew who had really killed Ben and that it wasn't Terry. So it was either someone who'd threatened her or someone she wanted to protect.

Candy had a memory of the way Mike had stood by the TV. He had glared at Adam, as if he was forbidding him to talk when PC

Edwards had been asking questions. Adam had looked even more frightened then than Tanya did now. It was only afterwards that he'd taken out the crumpled cigarette packet. Was showing that just a way of hiding everything he couldn't say about Mike?

The phone on the kitchen work-top rang. Tanya didn't move, not even to look up at Candy or the phone. She couldn't have been reading anything in the magazine because her eyes were still, staring at the same spot on the page.

Candy forced herself to pick up the phone and heard Mary's voice, sounding even more wobbly than normal.

She said, "They've arrested Terry. He's gone. They've taken him away."

Candy sagged against the kitchen work-top, not saying anything. Her relief about the arrest was mixed in with guilt for suspecting

Mike and worry about the way Tanya had lied about the knife.

"Are you there?" Mary said, after Candy had stayed silent for too long. "I said they've arrested Terry."

Candy coughed to clear her throat. Then she said into the phone, "That's great, Mary. Really great. But you must hate being on your own in the flat. D'you want to come and have something to eat here with Tanya and the boys and me?"

"I can't eat yet," Mary said. "Not with Ben … And I don't want to go out with a face like this. I'll be OK. Don't worry about me."

Candy said, "Whatever you want. But if you need us, just phone again. Tanya and I both want to help. I'm so sorry about Ben, you know."

"It's my fault," Mary said, with a horrible-sounding sob. "Like everything else. If I'd been stronger, Terry wouldn't have done it. Ben wouldn't be dead. It's my fault. I need ..."

"Mary, don't," Candy said. "You never hurt Ben. This is *not* down to you."

Mary sobbed once more, then laughed with a high, teetering sound that sent goose pimples all over Candy's arms. She wished Mary wasn't always so humble. The only thing that was really her fault was letting Terry come to live with her and Ben in the first place.

Tanya dropped the magazine as Candy put the phone down.

"Cheer up, Candy," she said. Tanya's voice wasn't normal either. It sounded strained. "Everything's going to be OK. Now, can you keep an eye on Mike for me later? I've got to go out tonight."

Chapter 9

CCTV

DS Smith took Terry down to the custody sergeant. But before they could get him into a cell, Smith was sent for, by DCI Blake.

Smith told Terry to wait with the custody sergeant, then ran upstairs to her office. DCI Blake was standing behind her desk, looking more angry than he had ever seen her.

She said, "Why didn't you check with me before you arrested him?"

Smith was surprised at the rage in her voice. Smith said, "Because Mary told the truth at last. Terry stabbed Ben. And he must have used the kitchen knife like I thought. A witness saw it there only yesterday morning and now it's gone."

DCI Blake folded up the file on her desk and said, "Mary was lying if that's what she said. And probably your witness was lying too."

Smith sat down heavily in the dark red chair by DCI Blake's desk. *It's the colour of dried blood*, he thought.

He said, "How d'you know?"

"The CCTV films from the estate show Terry couldn't have killed Ben," DCI Blake said. She looked sorry for Smith but still angry. "The tape shows Ben running away from the flat, quite safe," she went on more kindly. "Then it shows Terry leaving the flat about fifteen minutes afterwards, just as he said he did in his first statement."

Smith wanted to swear. Instead he said, "So maybe he didn't stab Ben in the flat. Maybe he had the knife in his pocket and did it when he found Ben hiding near the bins."

"That's not likely," said DCI Blake. "We logged the 999 call Terry made only two and a half minutes after he was first seen on the CCTV film. The paramedics got there seven minutes later. The size of the wound makes them think Ben had been bleeding for a lot longer than nine and a half minutes."

As Smith listened to DCI Blake, he thought how stiff and upright her small figure was. In every way she was the absolute opposite of Candy, whose loose clothes and easy stance did nothing to hide her amazing body. But he couldn't think of Candy now.

DCI Blake said, "You have to let Terry go. We haven't any evidence."

"Shit," Smith said. "So if it wasn't him, then who? One of the four bullying kids at school?"

"They each had an alibi that checked out," said DCI Blake.

Smith felt a pain right across his back, as though someone had tied it up with wire. He was tired, too. He said, "So we're back to square one."

The DCI nodded, "That's right. But there's not much more we can do tonight. Get off home and get some sleep. We'll start again in the morning."

Smith set off towards his flat, then started thinking about Candy and how she'd looked at him. He'd had an idea then that there were things she'd wanted to tell him. Maybe if he saw her on her own, she might talk. He turned round and headed back towards the estate.

Chapter 10
Bad Dreams

Later that night, Candy turned over and plumped up her pillow, asking herself what on earth she was doing. She'd only known Smith for a few hours. She never had sex with men she hardly knew. She hated one-night stands. She must have been mad.

He moved in his sleep, his hand reaching towards her over the white duvet. She couldn't help herself – so she took it in hers.

His eyes opened, widened in surprise, then crinkled in the smile she was coming to know.

"I didn't mean to fall asleep," he said, pulling her hand towards his face and rubbing his stubbly cheek against it. "Did you mind?"

"I liked it," she said telling the truth, glad he wasn't the kind of man to leap out of bed at the first possible moment. "It's been a long time since I've woken without feeling lonely."

He pushed himself up and stroked the tangled blonde hair away from her face.

"A woman like you?" he said. "I don't believe it."

"I don't tell lies," she said, and kissed him. Then she heard Adam crying out through the wall and flung back the duvet.

"He has bad dreams," she said. "He needs me. I'll be back as soon as I can. Don't go."

She dragged her dressing gown off the hook and put it around her body as she ran to sit on the edge of Adam's bed and tell him it was OK. There was nothing to worry about. Nothing. He was safe at home and in bed.

It took nearly ten minutes to get him alright again so that she could leave him alone. Then she trailed back to her room, hoping Smith wouldn't ask any questions. Even though they'd just made love and she knew she could trust him with everything about herself, he was still a police officer. And there were things about other people she couldn't tell him.

Smith was dressed and zipping up his leather jacket when she got back to her room. But the look in his eyes made her smile. He was like a little boy who'd been caught stealing apples.

"I'd better go before he works out I'm here," he said. "That would give any kid of his age bad dreams."

"You could be right," Candy said, wishing he wasn't.

"Can I come back tomorrow," he said, "if I promise to wait till he's asleep?"

She wanted to cling to him and beg him to stay for ever. But she couldn't, so she tried to make a joke of it and laughed, saying, "If you don't, I might kill you."

He laughed too and kissed her.

Chapter 11

Threats

Tanya was sweeping the balcony when Candy and Adam came out of the flat after breakfast next morning.

"Mike's already left for school," Tanya said. "You'd better run, Adam. You should catch him up if you're quick."

He looked up at Candy, as if he was worried about leaving her on her own. She gave him a quick smile and sent him on his way. If Tanya wanted to talk to her on their own, she must have something serious to say. Candy didn't even start to unlock her bike. She just leaned against the black mesh fence and waited.

Tanya laid down her brush and lit a cigarette, saying, "All right, Candy?"

"What d'you mean?" said Candy.

"I saw that DS Smith leaving your flat last night," Tanya said. "Creeping out like a thief at two o'clock this morning. I'd never have thought it of you. Well, not so soon, anyway."

Candy tried to laugh. "It seemed like a good idea at the time."

"Did he ask you about Mary's knife again?" Tanya said.

"No. Thank God. I don't know what I'd have said if he had. I wish you hadn't told that lie. He's not stupid. He'll ..."

Tanya took a puff, then dropped the fag and stamped it out. "It's done. Over. Forget it. You need to ..." Tanya broke off as they heard the foot-steps of a heavy man climbing the stairs.

Moments later Terry reached the top, panting. His face was the colour of raw steak and his hands were shaking. Candy had seen him like this once before and she knew it meant he was about to get violent. She backed against the wall, pressing her hands into the harsh grey concrete.

Tanya ignored him. She didn't show any sign of being scared this morning. Candy envied her. Tanya started brushing the rubbish again, towards the steps so that she could push it down to the next floor. When her brush touched Terry's feet, she looked up, pretending to be surprised to see him.

"Can I help you, Terry?" she said.

"Yeah," he said. "You can keep your fucking nose out of my business. Both of you. If I see either of you round our place, or talking to Mary anywhere on this estate, I'll see she never talks to anyone else ever again. Got that?"

He turned, without waiting for them to answer, and stomped back down the stairs.

Tanya swore, adding, "Did DS Smith say who they were going after next?"

Candy shook her head and bent to unlock the bike. She didn't want Tanya to know she thought it could be Mike.

"I've got to go," she said. "See you tonight, Tanya."

When Candy got to the office, the first thing she did was phone the number Smith had given her.

They said he wasn't there, but they wouldn't tell her where he was or how to get hold of him. All she could do was leave a message to say she'd called because she'd seen Terry in a temper and was worried about Mary's safety.

Chapter 12
Zero Tolerance

DS Smith walked into the incident room an hour later, after running through the options with DCI Blake.

DC Grant was checking more CCTV footage from the estate. He looked up and laughed.

"What's the joke?" Smith said.

DC Grant said, "You look well sorted. Got your end away last night, did you? I hear that Candy's been on the phone for you already this morning. Must have been a good night."

"Oh, fuck off," said Smith.

"We all know what you're like with women," Grant went on. "But I didn't expect even you to be giving her one so soon. Does the DCI know?"

Smith gave him a dirty look and turned away. He wished he'd told Candy not to phone him here. But then she didn't know what this bunch were like.

DC Grant was still laughing. "Edwards can't stop talking about her," he said. "Thick blonde hair, great big blue eyes, an arse you could gaze at for days at a time, and long, long legs."

"Can't he?" said Smith, thinking it was a pretty good description.

But it wasn't enough to explain the way he was feeling about Candy now. Long legs and a great arse might make a man want to fuck her but not go back and fight her battles for her. He wasn't sure he could do it, but he was damn well going to try.

"I didn't notice the arse or the legs," Smith said, lying. "Did she say what she wanted when she phoned?"

DC Grant didn't answer, but one of the others piped up, "She said she'd heard Terry making threats and was worried about Mary."

"Sensible woman," Smith said. "No wonder she phoned. I wish you lot would grow up."

He checked his emails, then left the building. He knew Candy would be at work now, so he'd have to wait till later to see her. But there was plenty else to do. First he had to check on Mary, then he thought he might go back to Tanya to find out if she had lied about the knife like DCI Blake had thought.

It wouldn't do any harm to have another go at the school, too. The four kids they had brought in yesterday might all have an alibi for the time Ben was killed, but there were plenty of other kids. Even if none of them had touched Ben, one of them must have seen – or heard – something.

When Smith got to Mary's flat, she wouldn't talk to him. He understood why as soon as Terry came rushing out of the living room, shouting, "Stop fucking bothering us."

Smith didn't move. Someone had to stand up to this bastard.

"We may have let you go for the moment," Smith said, "but that doesn't mean you're off the hook. And if you hit Mary again, we'll be back."

Terry gave him the finger and spat. "Get out of my fucking face."

Smith walked away.

Tanya was out – or at least wouldn't come to the door – so he went back across the estate to the school. First, he talked to the head teacher, Mrs Gordon, and told her what he wanted.

"I told your colleague none of the four could have done it," she said.

Smith could tell right away that she was the sort who distrusted the police. Maybe she'd never been attacked or robbed. She'd take a different line then. Do-gooders like her always did.

"I know they give some of the weaker ones a hard time," she went on. "But it's never been as bad as some of the parents claim."

"Tell me more about Ben," Smith said. "Was he one of those victims who provoke bullying even though they hate it?"

"We don't buy into that theory here," Mrs Gordon said. Now she looked as if she disliked him personally, not just his job. "We have a zero tolerance policy, and we make it clear it's always the bully's fault. In fact ..."

"Are you sure about the zero tolerance?" Smith said, remembering all the things Candy and Tanya had told him about the way Adam and Ben had suffered.

Mrs Gordon looked right at him. "Yes. This is a tough area, and a tough school. But whenever we catch any boy – or girl – bullying someone else we take action."

Her gaze shifted away from him as she added, "We don't always see everything, of course. And we can't be responsible for anything that happens beyond the school gates."

"No," Smith said. "Of course not." He couldn't help sounding sarcastic. He knew she knew what went on among her pupils.

"And you must be aware," she said, as if she was justifying herself, "that most children who bully have been victims too. Even little Ben …"

"Are you telling me Ben Jackson was a bully himself?" Smith said, aware that Mrs Gordon had said more than she'd meant. This could open up a whole new list of suspects.

"It only happened once," she said. She looked embarrassed. "It's not so surprising. It's what he's seen all his life, after all."

"What d'you mean?" said Smith.

"He hit a girl," said Mrs Gordon. "Just as his mother's boyfriend hits his mother. That's how it goes. They act out what they've seen."

"What happened?" Smith asked.

"One of his classmates went a bit too far when she was teasing him," said Mrs Gordon. "He lost his temper and thumped her. It wasn't a bad blow in itself, but she fell and cut her head. There was a fair amount of blood. She had to have a couple of stitches."

"When was this?" Jim said. His own blood started pumping faster. He could feel it in all the veins in his head. "Why didn't you tell us before?"

"Because it happened at the end of last term," said Mrs Gordon. "I didn't think it had anything to do with his death."

"You have to tell us everything," Smith said, wanting to shake some sense into her. "Is the girl in school now?"

Mrs Gordon turned away to check her records. "Yes."

"I need the name," Smith said.

Mrs Gordon raised her eyebrows, looking at him as if he'd been sent to her for bad behaviour. He didn't blink. He hadn't been frightened of a woman since he'd left primary school.

"She's called Sarah Davies. She's eleven, but she's in the same class as Ben was. Smarter than him, you see. She'd picked him as her number one target at the start of last term. I sometimes thought she was like a midge with him. But I am perfectly certain that she would never have taken any physical action against him."

"What d'you mean, like a midge?" said Smith.

"You know how they buzz around, then bite you and fly off out of reach before you can swat them. She was like that."

"And then one day Ben did swat her," Smith said, feeling some satisfaction on Ben's behalf. "I'll need to talk to her. You can be present if you want, and I'll get a police woman over to make her feel more comfortable."

"I'd rather not take her out of class," said Mrs Gordon. "Can you wait until lunch-time?"

"OK," Smith said, ready to give her that much help. "But tell me now, what kind of girl is she when she's not playing at being a midge?"

"Fine. We've had no problems with her. She does her homework, speaks up in class. Not badly behaved."

"A girly girl?" Smith said. "Or a tom-boy?"

"She's quite sporty," said Mrs Gordon. "And she probably has more friends among the boys than the girls, if that's what you mean."

"More or less," Smith said. "Has she ever been seen with a knife at school?"

"Indeed not," said Mrs Gordon. "We don't allow knives in school. Now, I must get on. I'll be ready for you when classes break for lunch."

As he left her cramped office, Smith saw Adam waiting outside a closed door further along the passage. Adam's trousers had a rip over the left knee, and there was ink on his shirt. They'd obviously been at him again.

Smith walked nearer and said, "Hi, Adam. How are you doing?"

Adam looked very pale and he began to stammer a bit. Then he said, "My teacher sent me to see the nurse. My head hurts and I can't see properly, so I can't work. Don't tell my mum, will you? She'll only worry."

84

Smith said, "OK. But I need to talk to her about something else. What time does she get back from work?"

Adam said, "Half past four. Sometimes she's late if her boss makes her do extra stuff. But most days it's half past four. I've got her mobile number if you need to speak to her now. She said I should always phone if it was important."

Smith said, "Great."

He wrote down the number, then left Adam to wait for the nurse.

Outside in the sunlight, Smith found an empty bench and sat down. He could see the river from here and he heard sea-gulls crying as they flew on the wind.

The air was cold, but it felt fresh on his face. He liked that. And his leather jacket was thick enough to keep him warm. He zipped it up.

He phoned Candy. When she answered, he said, "I got your message and I've been round to talk to Mary. But she didn't want to say anything. And I need to talk to you."

"Any time," Candy said, and her voice was as soft as it had been last night when he'd slid into her and felt her move under him.

He laughed, even though he didn't feel comfortable. "I mean, talk to you as in ask you some more questions about what goes on at school. There's not much time. Can we meet near your office?"

Candy rustled some papers, then she said, "Better not. You never know who's listening round here. I haven't got too much work today. I could leave a bit early. D'you want to come to the flat at half past three?"

Smith said, "Sure. I'll be there."

He put the phone back in his pocket and walked back to the police station. On the way he passed a flower shop. There were flower-pots of white Christmas roses in the window, just like the one in DCI Blake's office. He'd buy one for Candy as soon as the case was cracked, but not till then.

That way no one could accuse him of trying to bribe the witness, whatever else he was doing to her.

Chapter 13
The Truth

Smith was sitting on the top step outside the flats on the fifth floor when Candy came round the last corner with her bike banging against her legs. He was wearing his tatty old leather jacket again. She'd never seen a sight she wanted more. As she let the bike drop, she felt the tyres bounce as they hit the ground. Rather like the way her heart was bouncing in her chest.

She thought of the things they'd said and done last night and how making love had blotted out some of the horror of Ben's death.

She didn't want to think about that any more, or try to work out who'd really killed the boy. All she wanted was to drag Smith straight back into her bed and never answer another question.

"Did Terry threaten you this morning?" he said. "Was that why you phoned?"

These weren't the questions she'd been dreading. She rested against her bike, letting herself see the concern in his eyes. He didn't look like a man who'd wanted a one-night stand. She let herself dream for a moment.

"Candy?" he said after a while. "Did you hear me?"

She tried to remember what he'd asked. Terry. That was it. Had Terry been frightening her?

"He didn't threaten us," she said. "But he told Tanya and me that he'd hurt Mary if either of us had any more to do with her.

That's why I phoned. I was scared for her. Not for me."

The bike felt very heavy as she lifted it again. She sighed, and Smith came down the stairs at once to take it from her.

He lifted it up as if it weighed nothing and ran up the last flight of stairs.

She followed, still breathless. Smith propped her bike against the mesh fence.

He turned to look out across the estate. He said, "I didn't notice how much you can see from here. More than any of the CCTV cameras."

Candy let her gaze follow where his finger was pointing, towards the bins where Ben had been found. He was right. If the killer had been chasing Ben with a knife, anyone standing on this balcony would have seen them.

Smith went on, as if he had a private line into her thoughts, "Do you think Mike and Adam could have seen something?"

Candy turned her back on the view. How to do this without lying? She knew that if she lied, that would be the end of any chance she had with him.

"They said not," she told him, which was true as far as it went.

Smith watched her and said, "But Adam screams in the night. Are you sure it's not because he saw who killed Ben?"

"He hasn't said anything to me," Candy said, trying to keep all thoughts of Mike right out of her mind so that he wouldn't guess what she suspected.

"Maybe he wouldn't if it was someone he knew – and liked," Smith said, making her want to shiver. "Has he ever talked to you about a girl called Sarah Davies?"

Candy was so surprised by the name that she couldn't make her brain work for a minute. Then she got it. The tough little girl with the very short black hair and the scabby knees.

"Sometimes," she said. "They like her. She plays football with them. She came to tea here once. Why?"

"She had a history with Ben," Smith said. "I can't go into it all now. But there's a girl who looks a bit like her in a corner of one of the CCTV films. We need to know more ..." He stopped, then added, "if we're to eliminate her from our enquiries."

Candy dumped her bag on the kitchen work-top. For the first time he sounded cold. She felt very sorry for Sarah and her family.

"What was she like when she was here?" Smith said.

"She didn't make a very strong impression," Candy said. "She and the boys ate everything there was to eat for tea, then they vanished into Adam's room. I didn't see them again until she left so I don't think I can help you. But Adam won't be long. He'll know more."

Smith nodded. "OK. But there's one thing she said that I'm sure you could help me with."

"I'll try, but I need tea first," Candy said at once, as a way of putting off having to answer any of the trickier questions. "Do you want some?"

He said, "Why not? Great. Thanks."

She made the tea and thought about sitting beside him, letting her elbow touch his for a moment. But in the end she took the other sofa and crossed her legs, trying to look relaxed.

Smith drank some tea, then wiped his mouth and put down the mug. He looked nearly as worried as she felt.

"When I asked Sarah if she could think of anyone who might want to kill Ben," Smith said, "she couldn't. She said no one ever tried to hurt him. They might tease him, and poke him a bit, but no one ever did anything really bad."

"That sounds fair enough," Candy said, wondering why he was taking so long to tell her what he really meant.

"So then I asked her if she knew of anyone who carried a knife at school, and she said, 'Only Adam'." Smith paused, then he went on, "Is that true? Does Adam carry a knife?"

Candy laughed. This was easy, too.

"It's hardly a knife," she said. "One of those old little mother-of-pearl folding things. A pen-knife. And he doesn't exactly carry it."

"But does he take it to school?" Smith said.

"Not any more," she said. "I took it off him. Honestly, it's nothing to worry about. It's barely the size of my little finger."

Smith said, "Can I see it?"

"Why?" she said and was shocked to hear how aggressive she sounded.

Smith waited for a moment, then said in a low voice, "I could get a search warrant, you know."

Candy pushed some of her blonde hair behind her ears. She was wearing little gold studs in her ears. When she tugged at one it hurt her earlobe. She was glad of that. She hated to think how they'd been last night, when she would have done anything for him, when she'd been sure she could trust him.

She said, "Adam only got out the knife because he was afraid of the people who killed Ben. He wasn't going to hurt anyone with it. He couldn't."

Smith stood up and coldly said he needed to see the knife now.

Candy flinched at the sound of his voice and at the look in his eyes. He was staring at her as if they'd never met before. All the warmth she thought she'd seen in them had gone. She had trusted this man, slept with him, and now he was treating her like an enemy.

Feeling alone and desperate, she went into her bedroom to find the knife. She asked herself why she hadn't thrown it away at once. That would have been the best thing to do. The safe thing. But now it was far too late.

She didn't want the police coming in here with a search warrant. Anything was better than that, so she got the knife from her bedroom.

When she walked slowly back into the living room, holding the knife, she saw that Smith had put on a pair of thin gloves. She could smell the latex from where she stood. She had to force herself not to gag.

Smith took the pen-knife and opened the tiny blade.

He looked up at her and said, "There's blood here."

Candy said, "I know. It's mine. When I took it off Adam, I cut myself."

She held out her left hand and peeled back the plaster. It hurt even more than tugging at her earring. But it meant Smith could see the thin jagged red line where the blade had slid into her flesh.

"That looks fresh," he said, still talking as if they were strangers. "When did you take the knife off him?"

Candy opened her mouth to answer, but her voice wouldn't work. He gave a shrug and pulled an evidence bag out of his pocket so he could drop the knife into it.

He said, "I'll have to take it for testing, you know. You may as well tell me – it was right after Ben died, wasn't it?"

"I ..." she began. "Please. I ..." She couldn't go on, and he didn't even try to help her.

Chapter 14

The Confession

Candy whispered at last. "But Adam was buying cigarettes when Ben died. You know he was."

Smith said, "I know. And I've checked it on the CCTV films. But it took a long time for Ben to bleed out after he was stabbed. Adam could have bought the fags after he'd stabbed Ben."

Candy put her hand on her neck. She felt as though she might throw up or faint.

She said, "Don't forget he had to come in here to take the money from my tin. That would have taken time. The tin's on the top shelf there in the kitchen."

She pointed to a red and gold tea caddy. Her hands were shaking. And she was silently crying. She pushed the tears away in anger, pressing the back of her hand into her eyes.

She said, "And he wouldn't ever hurt anyone. He's too gentle. That's his problem. He has to fight against his own nature to be tough enough to survive."

Smith said kindly, "I know. I'm having to do the same thing myself now. And this knife may have nothing to do with Ben's death. But I have to check to make sure."

Candy turned her head away from him. She said flatly, "Adam's coming. I can tell the sound of his foot-steps."

They both heard a key turning in the front door. A minute later Adam came rushing in, shouting, "Mum! Mum! Listen ..." Then he stopped talking as he saw the evidence bag in Smith's hand.

Smith said, "I see you know what this is. When did you last use it, Adam?"

Adam glared at Candy as if he hated her. Did he think she had told on him? She looked even more ill.

Smith said, "Adam, you must tell me when you last used the knife."

Adam shook his head. Candy moved closer to him, but he put out his hands to keep her off. "Leave me alone," he said.

Smith put the bag with the knife in it into his pocket. "We'll test this. If there's any of Ben's blood on it, we'll find it. You might as well tell me what happened."

Adam shook his head and his blond hair flapped like a scarf. Smith moved closer. He was so tall he loomed over Adam. He knelt down on the floor so that their faces were almost at the same level.

"I know you never wanted to hurt Ben," Smith said, in a matter-of-fact way, as though he was trying to make it easier for Adam to answer. "So tell me what happened. Was it an accident?"

Adam suddenly shouted, "It was his fault! He wouldn't have got hurt if he hadn't done it."

Candy started to speak, but Smith ignored her. He carried on talking to Adam. "What did Ben do?" he said.

Adam said, "He ran onto the knife. I didn't know it was him. I thought it was them. The bullies. They'd said they'd give me two minutes' start, then they were going to come after me and if they caught me they'd throw me over the bridge into the river. I was scared. I thought it was them. I didn't know it was Ben. So when I knew I couldn't run fast enough, I stopped and got the knife out of my pocket and just stood there, holding it out. And I shouted at them to keep off me. To leave me alone or I'd hurt *them*. Then I felt someone running into me."

Smith said, "Why couldn't you see it was Ben?"

Adam turned away. For the first time he looked guilty.

He said, "As soon as I knew I couldn't get away, I shut my eyes and kept them shut while I shouted. I thought if I couldn't see, it would be easier."

Candy felt as though someone had nailed her feet to the floor and poured icy water all over her. She couldn't move or speak. All she could do was keep herself upright and try not to let her thoughts drown her. She'd once suspected Mike of the killing. Now she knew it was her shy, kind son who was guilty. But she could understand how it could have happened.

She wished she'd gone against his orders and collected him from school. That way she could have stopped anyone threatening to throw him in the river. He'd nearly drowned once in the pool where she'd been teaching him to swim. No wonder he'd been terrified.

How will he ever get over this? she asked herself. *How will I?*

Smith stood up again and said, "Come and sit on the sofa, Adam. We can sort this out."

Candy said in a voice that sounded as though she had a mouth full of sharp ice chips, "I don't think you should say any more, Adam. Not ..."

But nothing could stop Adam now. He went on without even looking at her and talked directly to Smith.

"When I pulled my knife away, I had to look at it," Adam said. "I saw the blood, so I knew it had cut someone. But I didn't think it had done anything else."

Smith waited without saying anything. Adam went on, "He didn't scream or anything. He just looked at me and said I'd hit him.

That's when I knew it was Ben. But that's all it was. He was standing up and still talking. It can't have been me who killed him. But I knew I'd get into trouble because I'd cut him, so I found Mike."

Smith said, "And did Mike tell you what to do next? To get an alibi by stealing the money to buy fags? And to change the shape of this knife by scraping it on something? There are scratch marks all along the blade."

Candy suddenly realised what she had to do. She tried to sound tough and sure of herself when she said, "This has to stop until we've got a lawyer here. Adam, go into your room while I talk to DS Smith. I'll get your tea in a minute. OK?"

Adam bit his lip, then he nodded and walked very slowly out of the room. His dirty trainers slopped along the dark-blue carpet. He seemed very young and very small.

Candy turned on Smith. She felt as though she was the evil twin of the woman who'd made love with him only last night.

"You tricked him into saying all that," she spat. "You'll never make a case against him now."

"Leave that stuff for the lawyers," Smith said. "And think! I'm trying to save him."

"That's a joke," she said. "A sick joke."

Smith shook his head.

"There's so much I want to say to you," he told her, "but I can't while you look as if you hate me."

That's not the half of it, she thought. Aloud she said, "What d'you want to say to me?"

"That I wish you could understand," he said sadly. "If Adam doesn't face what he did to Ben now, he'll spend the rest of his life trapped by it. He'll wait for ever for someone to tap him on the back and accuse him. He'll never be able to become the man he should be. This isn't anything to do with you and me – or not much. I like him. I couldn't bear that to happen to him."

Chapter 15
The Trial

Months later, Candy sat in court through every minute of Adam's trial. Mary was there, too, sitting with Tanya every day. Candy had tried to talk to Mary, but there was nothing more to say. They both knew what had happened and why it had happened. No words could make it any better for either of them. Tanya told Candy that Mary didn't blame her, but that didn't help either.

Candy saw Jim Smith dozens of times a day, and every time she caught him watching her she felt as though insects were crawling all over her body. One lunch-time he came towards her, looking as if he wanted to talk. She turned away. If it hadn't been for him, Adam wouldn't be here, going through this hell.

Today's first witness was called into the box to give evidence in Adam's defence. She was a woman Adam's lawyers had found, old and shaky but sure of the fact that she'd seen Ben on the afternoon he died.

Mrs Carter looked about 80 years old and her voice shook as she took the oath and told the court who she was.

Adam's lawyer asked what she had been doing on the afternoon of Ben's death. She said she had been walking home to her flat with her shopping when Ben came running past her.

"What did you see next?" asked the lawyer.

"I saw him chasing after a smaller boy and shouting. I wasn't surprised the smaller boy kept running away. I would have been scared of the shouting, too."

Adam's lawyer asked if she could see the smaller boy in court. She pointed to Adam.

His lawyer said, "Thank you, Mrs Carter. What happened then?"

The old woman said, "Ben shouted again and the other boy ran even faster, tripping sometimes but always getting up and running on again. He looked frightened for his life. Ben went after him and grabbed his left arm. The other boy turned round. I wasn't close enough to see what they did then. But after a moment, the other boy ran away again."

The lawyer said, "What did Ben do then?"

Mrs Carter said, "He turned and walked away in the opposite direction."

The lawyer asked her if she was sure she had seen Ben upright and walking.

"Oh, yes," she said.

The lawyer said, "Did he look as if he'd been hurt?"

"No," said Mrs Carter. "He was walking like any healthy young boy."

Candy could have kissed Mrs Carter. Her evidence supported everything Adam had said to Smith on the day he took the knife away for testing.

But they weren't finished yet. The lawyer for the prosecution stood up and started to ask his own questions, trying to make her say her eyes weren't good enough or that she'd made up her story.

She was strong enough to resist. Nothing he said made her change her mind. In the end, he had to let her leave the witness box.

When Mrs Carter had stepped down, the two lawyers made their closing speeches and then the judge started his summing-up.

He ran through all the evidence they'd heard over the last three days and then explained to the jury that they could only convict Adam of murder or manslaughter if they believed there was enough proof that he had intended to kill or harm Ben.

If they did not, he said, or if they believed Adam had acted only in self-defence, they had to give a verdict of not guilty.

Candy could not focus on the formal words. But she knew what they meant because the lawyers had explained what would happen.

At last the judge stopped talking and the jury went out to consider their verdict.

Adam was taken away. Candy could not bear to sit in the stuffy court, with Mary sitting only a few feet away. She had to get out.

She walked outside and was amazed to find the sun shining in a bright blue sky. A flurry of starlings chattered to each other as they flew round above the trees. She thought it would have been better if the sky had been black with rain clouds and the only sound had been the growl of thunder.

Smith was coming towards her. She turned her back on him.

He said, "Candy, don't. I know how you must feel, but I need to talk to you."

She said, "You don't know I feel. You couldn't. And *I* don't want to talk to *you*."

He said, "I haven't ever stopped thinking about you. I've wanted to phone every day. If I could have changed this, I would have. You must know that."

She didn't believe him. She wanted to tell him she'd fight for the rest of her life to stop thinking about the one time they'd made love.

He said, "Adam has a very good chance, you know. They may not convict him of either murder or manslaughter."

Candy said, "And if they don't, will you come after us again?"

He shook his head.

"What'll it be next time?" she said, not believing him. "A charge of possessing an offensive weapon? Or perverting the course of justice for me, Tanya and Mike? Or something else I haven't thought of in even my worst dreams?"

Smith said, "This is as far as it'll go. And whatever the judge decides to do with Adam, he will get through it, Candy."

She said, "No thanks to you." Then she turned away.

Chapter 16
The Verdict

Candy had been sitting on her bench for so long that she felt pins and needles in both her legs. She nearly missed the verdict. It was only because Smith came running to call her back that she got to her seat in time.

The foreman of the jury stood up. Candy gripped her hands together. There was a humming in her ears. She couldn't hear what the usher said to the foreman. She leaned forwards, over the empty seat in front of her, and tried to make her ears work. They missed most of what the usher was saying, but she heard the only important words.

The jury found Adam not guilty of murder or manslaughter.

In the sudden silence in court, even the humming in Candy's ears stopped. It was as if time itself had come to a stand-still.

She knew she should be cheering. But all she could do was sink back in her chair as all the tension of the last six months slipped away. She felt as though her legs were made of rubber. She wondered if she'd ever be able to stand up again. Her eyes felt wet and she realised she was crying.

Through the blur she saw Adam turn towards her. There was no triumph in his face either. She forced herself to smile. His lips trembled, then parted, and he was just able to smile back.

His lawyer came towards them to say goodbye. Candy took his hand between both of hers and tried to tell him how grateful she felt, but the words wouldn't come.

"I understand," he said. "It's been a bad time for you both. But it's over now. You must move on."

Candy started to say, "Without you, we'd never have ..." She could not finish her sentence. But she could see that he understood that, too.

When he left, she saw Smith. He'd been standing behind the lawyer.

"Candy, you probably don't ever want to see me again," he said. "But I just don't want to lose you. Or Adam."

She felt cold, then very hot, then icy cold again. Smith waited a moment, then he turned and put his hand on Adam's arm. Adam didn't pull away.

Smith said, "You did well. You spoke clearly, and everyone understood what had happened and why. It's all over now. Your life can start again."

Adam said, "Ben's won't."

At last Candy felt she could be proud of him again.

"I know," Smith said. "And we can talk about that later, if you want. But right now you need to forget about it and eat. I've never seen either of you so thin. Can I take you out for a pizza?"

Candy waited for Adam to make up his mind. It took a long time.

He looked at her, then up at Smith, then at his own feet. In the end he nodded and said, "OK. If you want."

Smith turned towards Candy and held out his hand. Adam's "OK" had given her permission to take it, but she wasn't sure if she could, or if she wanted to. After a while Smith let his arm drop to his side.

Candy looked away and saw Mary, standing with Terry. It was the first time she'd seen Terry since the day he'd threatened them on the balcony. He saw her and lurched forward, thrusting his face right into hers.

"So now you've got to admit it, you fucking cow! It was your toe-rag of a son who killed Ben."

Candy put her arm around Adam. He was trembling. She pulled him close to her side.

Terry was still shouting. "Now everyone knows I never touched Ben. Just like they know how you made Mary lie about me. She never wants to see you again. Not you nor your evil boy. So keep our of our fucking way. OK?"

Now Candy was shaking too. She wasn't sure now whether she was hugging Adam for his benefit or for her own.

Smith stepped between her and Terry. "No, you stay out of *our* fucking way," Smith said, making it clear that Candy and Adam were under his protection.

After a moment Terry took a step back, then he turned and stormed off. Smith took Candy's free hand. His skin felt warm against hers, and his strength helped her to control her shivering. She thought back to who he was and how she'd felt about him before he became Adam's enemy.

"Forget Terry," Smith said to her. "He won't touch you."

"I know," Candy said, "but ..."

"Forget him," Smith said again. "And come and eat with me. We've got a lot to say to each other."

"Please, Mum," said Adam.

She couldn't ignore that. At last she smiled and the three of them left the court together.

Want More? Why not try these?

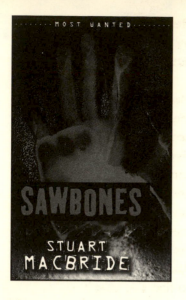

Sawbones
by
Stuart MacBride

They call him Sawbones: a serial killer touring America kidnapping young women. The latest victim is Laura Jones – the daughter of one of New York's biggest gangsters. Laura's dad wants revenge – and he knows just the guys to get it. Sawbones has picked on the wrong family ...

The Chop
by
Graham Hurley

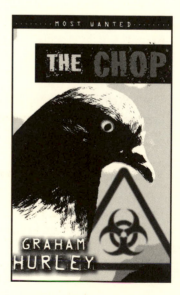

Bird flu has hit Britain. People are dying. The drugs don't work. Norman is just getting on with it. Helping out an old lady. Digging graves for bodies in the woods. Finding out dark family secrets. That sort of thing.
Just getting on with life ... and waiting for The Chop.

You can order these books directly from our website at
www.barringtonstoke.co.uk

Heroes
by
Anne Perry

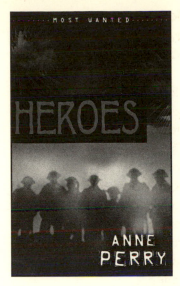

Murder on the battlefield. It's the First World War. Men are dying every day. Hundreds of them, sometimes thousands. But one death is different. One death is murder. How important is one murder among all the other dead? And how far will Joseph go to find the killer?

Kill Clock
by
Allan Guthrie

The kill clock is ticking ... Pearce's ex-girlfriend is back. She needs twenty grand before midnight. Or she's dead. She doesn't have the money. Nor does Pearce. And time's running out. Fast ...

You can order these books directly from our website at
www.barringtonstoke.co.uk